To Hillview Studio Guests.

Welcome to Folkland.

Jenni Gudgeon x

Folkland Fables

Jenni Gudgeon

For Aase, who also saw fairies.

Text and illustration © 2018 Jenni Gudgeon
www.jennigudgeon.co.uk

ISBN: 978-198649-493-9 (hardback)
ISBN: 978-1-64255-572-1 (paperback)

All rights reserved. No part of this book may be reproduced or used in any manner without the express written permission of the publisher.

Cover design: Inspired Cover Designs
Interior design: Polgarus Studio

To whom it may concern,

If you're reading this, you see Faerie's creatures.

You're not the first fairy-seer to exist and I doubt you'll be the last. I've told the gnomes to hand you this book when you're ready to learn more.

I'm the current custodian of Folkland Wood, and unlike the fairies, I won't live forever. I've written this book to describe all the characters who live here in case I'm gone by the time you arrive. You have to decide whether you want to follow in my footsteps.

It's scary when you realise other people don't see the creatures you do. I had no one to help me and think my life would've been easier if I'd had practical advice from someone who'd lived this way before.

Feel free to add your own notes and illustrations to mine. Fairies love their secrets, so there are always new mysteries to solve. My hope is for this field guide to grow through our joint experiences and help future generations of Folkland's fairy-sighted.

Hidden deep in the heart of Folkland Wood there lies a doorway into Faerie. It only opens when the moon grins mischievously in the sky, and even then, it's not open long. I've never gone through it myself, but those who have are awe-struck by Faerie's glamour and beauty. However, they're all weirdly affected by their experience, so I decided to stay home. Are the wonders behind the door worth more than your humanity? You need to make up your own mind.

Some fairies come to Folkland Wood to escape the Shining Ones' anger. A few are tourists, stopping off to see the sights. We also get fairies who are confused about their journey, with no idea how to get home. Most have jobs here though, and travel back to Faerie as often as possible.

The name of Folkland's ancient town literally means "Land of The Fairy Folk". Its wood lies to the west; a lush, enchanting place, full to bursting with unseen creatures.

In Folkland's past, man and fairy lived side by side in friendship and respect, until non-seeing humans arrived. They were frightened by the strange ways of the townsfolk, so accused them of witchcraft: a crime which was used to justify some horrendous punishments.

To protect themselves, Folkland's human population pretended not to see fairies. This offended their friends, who faded from sight. Fairy-vision was lost, turning tales of magical creatures from memory into myth.

Once in a while, fairy-seers are still born in Folkland town, and I've spent my entire life enjoying many delightful encounters with the fairies of Folkland Wood.

Welcome to my world.

There's always something lurking in the shadows, and it's always something exciting.

If you want to make friends with a gnome, tread lightly upon the earth, and never EVER mention fishing rods. They are hardened eco-warriors who nurse the world's hurts; turning the tables on those who harm it.

Mankind has a reputation as planet killers, so gnomes don't like us much. They don't understand why we take, take, take, without giving back. Then again, neither do I.

Gnomes are a generous, caring race with curious minds and a wicked sense of humour. They've got too much skin for their bodies, which undulates in dramatic waves as they walk. It's truly a sight to behold.

Because gnomes live underground, Folkland Wood is jam-packed with their burrows and lookout posts. One tunnel is even used by humans, its hilarious gnome graffiti on show for all to see. If you're quiet, you might hear them through the walls, going about their business in adjoining burrows.

Gnomes were the first creatures to welcome me when I hesitatingly entered the wood on my own. They taught me fairy ways and introduced me to shyer inhabitants like the brownies.

I was treated straight away like a beloved friend; my arrival marked by a simple ceremony bestowing on me the "freedom to walk the tunnels". Their instant trust overwhelmed me, so I've dedicated my life to becoming a link between man and fairy. I wasn't asked to do this; nor is it expected of you.

I've seen gnomes distraught with grief over a felled tree and incandescent with rage about the poisoning of our planet. Yet at full moon, they drop their responsibilities to host raucous parties in the meadow. Everyone is invited to drink the gnomes' delicious heather beer, before dancing together till dawn.

I always know it's going to be an amazing day when I stumble across the giant colony. I even go looking for them when I'm upset because it's impossible to feel blue in the company of giants. I'm greeted with gigantic hugs and huge smiles, like I'm the most important person in their lives. Everyone is welcomed this way. They are affectionate creatures with a compelling need to include the whole world in their happiness.

Giants are like overgrown toddlers. They love to have fun and play games - especially Sardines. Sometimes they stay hidden for days, all cramped up together, trying not to giggle as people walk past.

Unfortunately, like all infants, giants have occasional temper tantrums where they pull up a few trees. This is the only time they're dangerous. Keep an eye on their mood, and distract them if you see one getting confused. At the same time, be prepared to run for your life. I've broken bones when a diversion failed.

Giants are surprisingly hard to find, despite their size. They know all the best hiding places and are experts at camouflage. Too good really: I'm convinced they use magic to disappear. They constantly deny this accusation, while smiling sneakily at each other. It's cheating. Maybe you can get them to stop?

The only thing that frightens giants is the wind, so check the weather forecast daily. If it's stormy, the fachans will help gather the colony together in a safe place. Fairy folk still talk about the terrible night the giants forgot to hide. An impressive lightning display distracted them, until they panicked at the wild weather and began to rampage. In the morning there was scarcely a tree left upright near the tower on the cliff. The giants were in disgrace for weeks.

Faerie is ruled by the Shining Ones, who in turn are ruled by the Faerie Queen. The Shining Ones are extremely tall, fascinated with humans, and appear to glow from within. They leave no trace when passing by, except a tinkling echo from the bells wound through their hair. They scare me witless.

The Shining Ones will enchant you, if possible, so your life revolves around pleasing them. You always see a few entrapped humans in their company, who are treated like toys: played with, praised, then tortured till they break.

In olden days it amused the Faerie Queen to interfere with our monarchs. The kings and queens met her regularly in Folkland Wood, where she encouraged them to build spectacular mansions in which to entertain her.

The brownies told me she laughed contemptuously when she saw the palace in Folkland, refusing to enter "such a ramshackle mess". Bricks and stone can't

compete with magical buildings. She'd maliciously enjoyed watching them beggar the country to try and impress her.

The Faerie Queen usually brought with her to Folkland a human nicknamed "the Rhyming Man". He walked around town proclaiming his rambling poetic nonsense, followed by royal scribes jotting down his every word. Humans sometimes see the future after living in Faerie, so the man's gobbledegook contained several valuable prophecies.

The Shining Ones are rare visitors to Folkland these days. If they appear during your lifetime, stay close to a fairy friend until you're officially sanctioned. I still tremble at the memory of my encounter with the Faerie Queen. I felt my soul rush into her, until all I had left was a longing to follow her to the end of the worlds.

I would have become her plaything if the ghillie dhu hadn't pleaded for my life. The queen eventually got bored and dismissed us, lazily granting me safe passage.

Fachans (pronounced fac-anns) are tiny, aggressive shamen with one arm, one leg, and one eye. They are mystics who spend a lot of time in a trance. It's infuriating to watch them drift off during a conversation, especially when they're in the middle of a sentence.

Our fachans live in a mossy hollow near the witch's cave. Their camp is heavily guarded because it protects three sacred stone balls, which they'll defend to the death. They attack first, ask questions later, and dislike strangers, so take along a fairy friend on your first visit. Actually, it took me a long time to build a good relationship with the fachans, so I wouldn't visit them at all unless you decide to join the fairy community.

After ten years or so, the fachans might show you their sacred stones. I've been lucky and have seen them three times. It's an uncanny experience, which removes you from your body, before being scattered into the surrounding air. The fachans won't tell me what the stones do to them or let me see the stones again. Three times is enough for symmetrical people.

Every fairy takes their turn to help fachans train against any potential invasion to steal the stones. Fachans work together like a single creature, swarming over thieves while bombarding them with cursed apples. The giants are thrilled when it's their turn, saying it tickles. The shellycoat hates it.

Fachans are desperate to take over the world, though I've never learnt why. They'll earnestly debate any new plan, so I spend far too much time dreaming up crazy schemes to offer as suggestions. It's hard not to laugh at how seriously they take my proposals, huddling together, solemnly considering the pros and cons, until one fachan dejectedly explains to me why it won't work. I pretend to be astonished and promise to keep trying.

Unicorns leave a dazzling display of stars and flowers wherever they go. This tells you exactly when to head off in a different direction. They are vain, stupid, creatures who hate lions and are obsessed by the length of their horn.

It used to bother me that unicorns' personalities aren't as beautiful as their appearance, until I understood what they'd gone through. We'd all become big-headed if we were told "you're perfect in every way" for centuries. I feel deeply sorry for them, but they still annoy me.

Every solstice, unicorns meet for a Blessing at the ruined temple on the wood's southern border. This ceremony is supposed to give thanks for how lucky they are to be so perfect, although it quickly descends into loud declarations about how fabulous they are.

Blessings always end up becoming a tallest-horn competition. I refuse all invitations

now because I'm asked to judge. Unicorns stand on their hind legs (which make their horns higher), show off their profile, and you pick the tallest. Simple. Except all unicorns not picked will sulk for weeks, sometimes months, occasionally years. The shellycoat is their usual judge. She's the kindest, most compassionate of us all.

As soon as unicorns mention lions, change the subject – try anything! I've listened to them rage on about lions for hours, repeatedly declaring how they "can't understand how these awful animals exist". Then they ask if you think their tail looks like a lion's tail. Don't hesitate, just lie. Say no and get away as quickly as possible.

I've never found out whether unicorns are dangerous to humans. Until I do, I refuse to provoke anyone with an intimidating horn sticking out of their forehead.

All fairy woods are protected by a ghillie dhu (pronounced gil-ee-do). They are small, well-camouflaged creatures, who wear necklaces full of polished baby teeth.

That sounds little creepy I know, yet our ghillie isn't scary at all. He helps lost children and ensures the dryads (tree spirits) are content.

Dryads' faces show on their tree trunk, so they're easy to spot. Your hair stands on end when touching the bark, and they sprout delicious mushrooms in May.

Trees sleep in winter, which makes the dryads sluggish. The ghillie dhu visits each dryad every day to keep their minds active. Dryads control the emotions of the wood. If they become drowsy, the whole community loses its focus: tempers fray, friendships strain, and fights break out.

Our ghillie travels all over Folkland Wood, except the beech hedges path. I used to tease him mercilessly about it before realising I did the same. I've no idea why. Have

you noticed anything unusual about this path? I feel sick even thinking about it.

The ghillie dhu was my best friend when I was young. We spent my entire childhood climbing trees, singing birdsong, trailing animals, and foraging for treats. However, ghillies don't like adults. As I grew up, he turned away from our friendship. Now he snarls when he sees me, shouting to "Keep away" from my dryad friends.

So make the most of your years with him. He'll protect you, charm you, and become your closest companion. But always be aware of time passing. You've got no other choice than to become someone he detests.

I am still angry, upset and confused because my best friend hates me.

Kelpies are shape-shifting waterhorses with an unfortunate habit: they drag children into deep water for their lunch. Our kelpies live in the pools beyond the waterfall, so stay away from there until you're over eighteen. It's probably worth keeping an eye out for hoofmarks around other secluded ponds as well, just in case.

On land, kelpies look like docile, friendly ponies, the perfect size for exhausted children to ride home on. The child only realises how wet the pony is when they touch it. By then it's far too late. Their hand is stuck fast, and they're being dragged towards water, while the placid pony transforms into a hideous, galloping beast.

When I was young, kelpies shrieked at me: "Stay away!" and "Don't touch!" They shout this to every child, yet despite their obvious anxiety, fairy magic changes the frantic pleas into fascinating words of welcome.

Kelpies don't want to be monsters. They are devastated by every single death, hating

themselves for being unable to stop the slaughter. I help the gnomes run group-therapy sessions to boost their self-confidence. We celebrate achievements, talk through failures, and desperately search for a solution.

Currently, I run tours for local schoolchildren round Folkland Wood. We make shelters, play games, and have fun, before I warn them about the dangers. I especially mention our rare breed of carnivorous pony who attacks to kill if approached. I show photos, along with an unnerving film depicting a mocked-up assault.

We've not had a death for a few years now, though word seems to have escaped about our incredible ponies. Bewildered people from around the world contact me for more details. I write back with convoluted tales of mythical creatures and never hear from them again.

Will-o'-the-wisps are floating spirits, normally seen as spooky lights glowing deep in the undergrowth. They pop out when you're not quite sure where to go and are always determined to help.

Don't go with them though, because wisps are unpredictable creatures. Occasionally they'll lead you to exactly the right place, but usually you're enchanted into following them for miles. I thought wisps were my friends, even believing it was a mistake the first time I found myself tired, muddy, and stuck fast in a bog. I woke from my enchantment as the giggling wisp disappeared in a puff of smoke.

They remind me of childhood bullies who demand to be friends one day, only to be horrible to you the next. You can't even ignore them. If you don't follow them, they hover over you, blowing the most descriptive raspberries. They time the raspberries to your steps, so everyone comes out to watch, like it's a parade.

    I put on a show for them. Fluttering on tiptoes to the spluttering, wobbling my bottom to explosions, and generally acting the clown. Although it's embarrassing to be the centre of attention, it's better to laugh with people than be laughed at by them. As a bonus, wisps hate being upstaged. They go in a huff before slinking back into the darkness, leaving me to take my applause.

    The wisps meet with flower fairies every Sunday night, at the massive pillars near the talking stones. I suggest you keep well back if you investigate; I've received several bitten noses while spying on them. And take a coat. To deter visitors, they conjure up a freezing cold dome for half a mile around.

I don't know how wood brownies see anything, because they have dark holes instead of eyes. They've been cursed to clean Faerie territories till everything is "spick and span, with each leaf neat in its place."

This ridiculous punishment was handed down to an entire species after one single wood brownie laughed at a Shining One when it stumbled, thousands of years ago. You don't laugh at the Shining Ones.

I adore brownies. Their job is completely pointless, yet they have bright, rewarding lives by playing "Tell the Tallest Tale" while they work. I often join the cleaning, where I am ordered to take my turn, even though I'm not a great storyteller. I recount the true-life tales of eccentric humans across the world which I plunder from newspapers and magazines.

Brownies tidy the wood in an anti-clockwise spiral from the outside edge to its

core. To find them I follow their leaf-polished trail. This spiral can be seen everywhere, so it must be an important mystical symbol.

I asked the brownies what it means, but you may notice they talk a lot without saying very much, so I'm none the wiser. If you learn anything relevant from their conversation, please add it to this guide.

In winter months, wood brownies spend all their spare time researching ancient Faerie battles. These are re-enacted by Folkland's fairies at the annual carnival, entertaining countless creatures from many different worlds.

It's my favourite time of year. Overnight, the meadow fills up with fantastical tents starting the week-long festivities. The extravaganza flaunts the colour and music of Faerie culture, with irresistible dancing, unbelievable acrobatics, and mind-boggling feasts. This celebration provides inspiration for many a future story.

Shellycoats are extremely lanky, with large eyes and frog-like mouths. They wear riverweed cloaks full of shelled creatures who gorge on the fungus shellys cover themselves with. The molluscs ooze all over the shellycoat, creating a horrendous stink which attracts midges – a shellycoat's favourite snack.

Folkland only has one shellycoat left, after the others disappeared one night in peculiar circumstances. Our remaining shelly is a gentle, relaxing companion, who stays close to the wiggly path leading to the waterfall. She spends most of her time cheering up the nearby kelpies. When I want to see her, I follow the line of slugs and snails that pursue her wherever she goes.

Shellycoats love practical jokes, and will rope in assistants if possible. Expect to join in her fun if you decide to continue as a fairy-seer. She pleads with those enormous eyes, making it hard to say no. Her favourite trick is completely ridiculous; everyone

just pretends to fall for it to make her happy.

First, the shellycoat slides into the steep-sided pool under the waterfall. Next, she splashes loudly while shrieking for help. That's my cue to run around in a panic, shouting for people to come and rescue her. When my group arrives, the shelly skips merrily off down the stream, shells a-jangling, laughing wildly to herself. We whoop and cheer, which she acknowledges with a wave of her hand before disappearing into the bushes.

Playing pranks makes the shellycoat deliriously happy, but her good mood doesn't last long. She feels driven to perform jokes she used to play with her family, which makes her miss them all the more. Afterwards, she goes off quietly by herself to grieve; just her, alone with her snails.

The flowers in Folkland Wood are more dazzling than elsewhere because they're cherished by fairies who live in them. Flower fairies move from plant to plant, depending on what's in bloom, twinkling particularly brightly on personal favourites.

These beautiful, insect-sized creatures become ugly and vicious when roused. Human scent makes flowers wilt, so they loathe us. If we get too close, they launch a frenzied attack, swooping down with blood-curdling howls before biting the intruder ruthlessly on the nose. It took me years to learn their nomadic calendar, so I could avoid walking past their seasonal homes.

Flower fairies are especially aggressive when living in primroses. On spring weekends, I wait with a first-aid kit at the pond near the entrance to the wood, ready to help the stream of bloody-nosed humans fleeing back to town.

The troll is one of the few individuals flower fairies trust. He persuaded them to

stop assaulting me if I stayed on the path. Apparently, my screams were unsettling him.

Now I'm allowed to study flower fairies, as long as I don't talk about what I see. Their work is top secret. It's a great opportunity to watch them go about their business, though I'm always accompanied by a guard who continually comments about my smell.

I'd like to tell you I've got magnificent secrets about this fascinating species which I'm unable to talk about. However, I've not learnt much about flower fairies from studying their habits close up. Sometimes I think I knew just as much before, when they were biting me. Maybe you can persuade the fairies to be more open. I haven't even discovered the answer to my first, most basic question: How does someone live in a flower?

Folkland's washerwoman is skeletally thin with one last remaining tooth. She has straggly hair, a sharp tongue, and predicts death by washing blood from the clothes of humans who are about to die.

Somehow, she also cleans blood from people's clothes whose later death is completely bloodless, though she won't tell me why: fairies love to be mysterious. Likewise, I've no idea where the clothes, or the blood, comes from. I don't even know how she gets the will-o'-the-wisps to act as clothes pegs for her on windy days.

She likes lonely places, so look for her along streams near the talking stones, on the wood's northern border.

Washerwomen are cousins to banshees who, according to her, "Get all the attention by screeching and moaning like maniacal fools." Washerwomen just pull up their sleeves to get on with the dirty work. I really admire that.

It's not like she doesn't complain though. I can listen to her rant about the workshy banshees for hours, grumbling that she does everything while "SOME PEOPLE never do nothing!" and "What's the use of all that wailing? It doesn't make blood come out any quicker!"

Don't be put off by her gruffness. The washerwoman likes an audience, even if she doesn't show it. When she wants to be alone, she shouts out this weird little speech:

"Don't you try to suckle me.

I know you lot. Sneaking up on a lady for a wish.

A wish? I'll give you a bleeding wish! I wish you'd push off that's what I wish."

I've never figured out what this means, but it's a good idea to take her advice. I once stayed with disgusting consequences. She got ruder and ruder until she threw the blood-stained clothes all over my head. Eurgh.

Every so often a gang of pucks arrives in Folkland Wood, and race around causing chaos. They're a similar height to hobbits, but act nothing like them. Pucks have rough fur, cruel grins, and consider nothing except their own amusement at other people's expense.

The pucks' favourite game is to pin drawings of lions onto trees. Unicorns charge at the lion, getting their horn stuck. Pucks then clamber all over the unicorn till a passer-by shoos them off, whereupon they flee to the top of nearby trenches making rude gestures at everyone.

I admit I chuckle to myself at the first stuck unicorn I see. They are extremely irritating. Soon though, I'm rescuing eight or nine unicorns a day from their own stupidity, which makes the joke wear rather thin.

Pucks are unkind to everyone, including me. When I spot their faces watching me

through the leaves, I go down on all fours. Then I contort my face to be as gruesome as possible and snarl. I sneak away while they're rolling round the floor, laughing uncontrollably at the kitten who thinks it's a tiger.

When pucks are elsewhere, they are talked of nostalgically, with much laughter about their craziness and tricks. Despite this, it's not much fun when they're here. The longer they stay, the more destruction is caused. Damaged trees from trapped unicorns; pulled-up flower-fairy homes. They even tear apart the washerwoman's cleaned clothes, flinging the pieces into trees. It's complete pandemonium.

Finally, the pucks are ordered to leave and never come back. This cycle happens over, and over again. You can't stop it; I've tried. No one will send the pucks off straight away, despite knowing exactly what will happen. It hurts that no one will explain why – maybe they'll tell you. Sometimes I feel very human among my fairy friends.

Every time I see our troll my heart breaks a little bit more. No goats trip-trap across his bridge near the meadow, so he's distraught in his hunger and despair.

He tried eating a couple of children once; they burned his throat horribly. He wept bitter tears while watching them run off home, covered head-to-toe in slimy yellow troll saliva.

If you must cross his bridge, it's a good idea to shout out as you approach. I hate watching the hope, which lights up his mismatched eyes, fade into misery when he realises he can't eat me. Each time I promise to find him a goat, but cross my fingers. Trolls are disgusting eaters.

Occasionally, the pucks forget the trouble they got into last time, and give him a goat. Trolls ripen their food before eating, so the area around his bridge becomes unbearable with the stench of decayed goat. They savour their meals by eating them

several times over; allowing the nuances of the meat's distinctive flavour to be fully appreciated. Regurgitated goat meat decorates the nearby trees for months on end.

I've never seen the troll all at once because he prefers to remain hidden. Normally I just see his eyes and fingers peeping through holes in his bridge. Yet, for one week a year, as winter turns to spring, he leaves his shelter every night. In the mornings, I spot his saliva trails glistening high in the tree-tops. I've no idea why he climbs up there. I stopped trying to stay awake and watch him after realising I always fell asleep on the dot of midnight.

Our troll is miserable, which upsets me. I've tried so many ways to make him happy (without goats) and I know I've failed. I'd be overjoyed if you succeed; it would be nice for us to have a happy troll.

Seeing fairies comes at a price. For me, the sacrifice was worth making; you need to decide for yourself. Fairy-sighted humans view two worlds at once, which shows in our faces. Un-seers are flustered by our difference, which can lead to violence. If this world becomes too unusual for you, feel free to say goodbye and walk away. Don't be afraid to admit it's too much. Others have left, to enjoy perfectly normal, fairy-free lives.

Hanging around fairies makes humans listless or away with the fairies for a short while afterwards. The more you visit Folkland Wood, the longer the fog takes to clear. If you travel into Faerie, you'll never be clear-headed away from that realm again.

I have a few human friends, who I socialise with inside the borders of the wood. They've accepted my dual personality and don't mention how dozy I become in town. These friends are important to me. People of my own species bring me back down to earth after spending my days among the supernatural.

It is possible to teach humans how to see fairies, but they don't let just anyone catch sight of them. Fairies are seen with your heart, not your eyes, so budding seers should be carefully selected. It's not an easy task and the people I've taught can only catch glimpses.

Candidates must respect all lifeforms, acknowledging every creature's place in the world. They are also required to learn how to tune out the busyness of the human world allowing the earth's beauty and mystery to shine through.

Now it's over to you. The fairies only let one in ten million children see them properly so whatever your decision, please remember you're special. This doesn't mean there is any obligation to follow a path chosen for you by others. Your life is still your own.

Good luck.

Acknowledgements

Enormous thanks to my husband and all my family. They were forced to go into raptures at my pictures and expected to laugh at all my stupid jokes.

I couldn't have written this book without help from my wonderful mentor, Sarah Painter. She was consistently encouraging and gentle while I learnt the basics of writing.

Thanks also to Lorraine McKendrick who taught me how to draw. She dealt with my tears when things went badly, and celebrated with me when pictures went well.

Thanks to all my friends, and my colleagues at Cupar library. They've been patiently waiting for this book for years, and have outwardly seemed excited at my progress.

Thank you also to those who read my semi formed manuscript and told me what they liked and what made no sense at all.

I love you all x

Animals to search for in each picture

A Bat

Bees
(try counting them all – I bet you can't)

Birds that visit my garden in Scotland
(this might be tricky; you probably haven't been to my garden.)

Butterflies; Caterpillars; a Chameleon; Dragonflies; a Frog
A Hedgehog; a Grasshopper; Ladybirds; Mice a Mole
(These are all peeking out from their holes except one – can you find it?)

Mushrooms
(Not exactly an animal, but not a plant either.
I decided it didn't matter - I like drawing mushrooms.)

An Owl; a Red squirrel; Snails; a Spider; a Tortoise

One animal in each picture is a homage to an animal in a famous children's book.

Some animals didn't want to be stared at, so they've sneaked off the page.
Cheeky wee mites!

Printed in Poland
by Amazon Fulfillment
Poland Sp. z o.o., Wrocław